Out

by

Joanna Kenrick

Illustrated by Julia Page

First published in 2010 in Great Britain by
Barrington Stoke Ltd
18 Walker St, Edinburgh, EH3 7LP

www.barringtonstoke.co.uk

Copyright © 2010 Joanna Kenrick
Illustrations © Julia Page

The moral right of the author has been asserted in
accordance with the Copyright, Designs and
Patents Act 1988

ISBN: 978-1-84299-764-2

Printed in Great Britain by Bell & Bain Ltd

A Note from the Author

I wrote this book because someone asked me to. "Being gay doesn't have to make you unhappy," he said. "Sometimes the problem is what other people think, not the fact that you're gay."

It's true – we often think that being different makes people unhappy. But it isn't always like that. I wanted to show a gay character who was happy being gay. And that the problems he faced were because other people didn't like it.

I wrote the story three times in three different ways before it worked. I wanted to write the story from Will's point of view, but I found it too hard. Maybe that says something about me as a person as well as my writing skill?

I am pleased with the final story. The person who asked me to write it likes it too, which is even more important. I hope you agree with both of us.

For Benjamin Franklin, with thanks.

Contents

Chapter 1

My Best Friend

It only hit me last week. I can't believe I didn't see it before. I was just sitting, talking with Will as I always do – and suddenly I knew. Right in my guts. It was a kind of warm feeling. I had to bite my lip to stop myself blurting it out right there and then.

I fancy you.

No, I didn't say it out loud. But in my head it was like a shout, it was so clear.

Will is my best friend. I've known him since I was about six, when he lived next door. He moved across town when we were ten, but we stayed best friends. My real name is Natalie but he called me Carrots, because of my hair. I called him Willy to wind him up.

It doesn't seem that long since we were little, but now we're both fifteen. I didn't ever think of him as a possible boyfriend. He was just Will.

But one day last week, we were sitting talking. He was waving his hands around as always. And I don't know why, but all of a sudden, I thought, *you're lovely. Where will I ever find someone as nice as you? And you're good-looking too. Oh, God, what am I going to do?*

Will looked at me. "You all right? You've gone a funny colour."

I had to look at the ground. I knew I was blushing. "I'm fine. Listen, I gotta get to class."

He looked at his watch. "We've still got ten minutes."

"Yeah, but I've got to – go to the loo."

He looked puzzled, and then he said, "Oh, right. Is it that time of the month?"

I muttered something and dashed off.

I hid round the corner until the bell went. My hands were shaking. Why did this have to happen? Why now? We were best friends! If I told him I liked him – fancied him – would he stop being my friend? What if he didn't want to talk to me any more?

And then, a tiny voice in my head said, *but what if he feels the same way?*

!!?!

Oh, my GOD what if ...?

But that was too scary to think of, so I crushed it down deep inside me and tried to think of something else.

Chapter 2
Tell Him

I tried to act normal, I really did. But
every time I saw Will after that, I got this
funny feeling in my guts. Almost like I was
going to be sick. And I started to notice
other girls looking at him, and I got jealous.
Jealous, me! But Will had always got on well
with girls. Most of his friends were girls,

come to think of it. Girls liked Will because he listened to them. He was good at listening. And he noticed if you were upset. He was always a good shoulder to cry on. Goodness knows, I'd cried on it myself lots of times.

But now, I didn't want to cry on his shoulder any more. I wanted to lay my head on it, kiss his neck, put my arms around him ...

Gaaah! Stop thinking about it!

I was half hoping that Will would spot that something was up with me. Like I said, he was good at seeing that kind of thing. But he seemed a bit unlike himself. Once or twice I saw him gazing across the class room with a weird look on his face. But there was only a group of boys over there – nothing odd about that.

Night after night I lay awake wishing I knew what to do. And then I saw a film. It was about a man who died before he got the chance to tell this woman he loved her. I cried buckets.

I made up my mind.

"Will," I said the next day. "Can I talk to you?"

He grinned at me. "Of course you can, Carrots."

"Don't call me that," I said in a sharp voice. "My name is Natalie."

He looked taken aback. "I know. But I've called you Carrots for years. You haven't minded before."

"Well, I mind now," I said. Then I felt bad. I didn't mean to start by telling him off.

"What is it?" said Will. He looked closely at me. "You OK? What's the matter?"

I pressed my hands together. *Come on, Natalie. You can do it. Just tell him.* "You know how we've been friends for ages? I mean, you know me better than anyone else."

"Yeah."

A boy walked past. Will looked round to see who it was.

I carried on. "And you've always said I can tell you anything, right?"

"Mmm," he said.

"Well," I said, and I took a deep breath, "the thing is, Will ..."

"Natalie," he said suddenly. "I think I'm gay."

Chapter 3

You WHAT?

I stared at him. "You – what – but I ... *what?*"

He swung round, and his face was white. "I can't keep it a secret any more. I have to tell someone. And you're my best friend."

"Yeah, but ..."

"And like you said, we can tell each other anything, right?" He suddenly stopped. "Oh, God, I'm sorry. You were in the middle of telling me something."

"It can wait," I said slowly. I couldn't believe what I was hearing. "You – you think you're gay?"

"I'm so sorry," he said again. "I haven't slept for weeks. I don't know what's going on with me."

17

I looked across the playground. The boy who had just walked past was talking to his mates by the tennis court. "That's Paul," I said. I looked back at Will. "Are you – looking at Paul?"

Will's face was so unhappy. "I can't stop thinking about him," he said and his voice shook. "It's crazy. I must be going mad. Mustn't I?"

It was like something inside me had stopped. Frozen. I shrugged my shoulders, trying to act normal. "I don't know."

"But when I look at him ..." Will's gaze went back to Paul. "When I see him – it's like my heart turns over. It makes me feel dizzy. Do you know what I mean?"

I closed my eyes. "Yes," I said. "I know what you mean."

"I've never felt that way about a girl," said Will.

I bit my lip. "Never?"

"Never." Will shook his head. "I guess – I mean – I suppose that means I'm gay, doesn't it?"

"I don't know, Will."

Suddenly he grabbed my arm. "Don't tell anyone, Natalie. Please. I'm not even sure, yet. Maybe it won't last?" He looked hopeful.

It was so hard to smile, but I did it. "Maybe it will go away," I said, and patted his hand, though my fingers burned at the touch.

"Don't worry, I won't tell anyone. Like you say, maybe it won't last."

He smiled back in relief. "Thank God I've got you, Carrots." He pulled my ponytail. "You keep me sane. What would I do without you?" Then he gave me a quick hug. "Catch you later, OK?"

"OK." I watched him run off – his school bag flapping against his long legs. That short brown hair that always fell over one eye. The hands that were always moving while he was talking. And I tried not to think about my poor heart and how it was breaking.

Chapter 4

That Night

I cried that night. It didn't help that Will kept texting me:

I'm so confused.

How do I know if I'm gay? Is it for life?

Do you think it's just Paul? Maybe I won't ever fancy any other boys. Maybe it's just him.

They say lots of people are mixed up about their feelings when they're teenagers. Maybe that's all it is?

Maybe Paul is mixed up too???

Do you think Paul would ever – erk, can't believe I'm saying this – go out with me??!

AM I GOING MAD??!!

I tried to text back, to be a good friend. I don't think he noticed there was anything wrong. But every text he sent made me cry, so in the end I sent him a text saying,

Going to bed, see you tomorrow.

He sent an instant reply.

Of course, good night. So sorry to be all me me me. You were trying to tell me something at break. I promise I'll listen tomorrow. Thanks for being such a good friend.

I switched off my phone and sobbed into my pillow.

Will thought he was gay. How could he have kept this a secret from me? How could I not have known?

If he *was* gay, it meant he would never feel the same way about me as I did about him.

And do you know what hurt the most? Thinking about what might have been. If I'd felt this way a year ago – if I'd asked him out *then* ... would he be gay now?

I pulled the duvet over my head and prayed that my heart would stop hurting soon.

Chapter 5

The Hurt

My heart didn't stop hurting over the next few weeks. In fact, it got worse, because the more I talked to Will, the more sure he became. He didn't fancy girls. End of story. I would never be his girlfriend. And that made me want it even more, and that made it hurt even more ...

And Will saw I was upset. "What's the matter?" he said, more than once.

"Nothing," I told him.

"You can tell me anything," he said. "You know you can. After all, I've told you my deepest secret."

"I know," I said. "It's nothing, really."

He shook his head, and I knew he didn't believe me. But how could I tell him? It would make everything worse.

Will was getting really screwed up over Paul. If I hadn't been in love with him, I might even have found it funny. He mooned over Paul like a teenage girl! "Did you see him play football today? Hasn't he got the fittest legs ever?"

I rolled my eyes.

"Oh, and did you hear this joke? Paul told it to me the other day ..."

In the end, I snapped. "Well, if he's so amazing, why don't you just ask him out?"

He took a step back in horror. "I can't do that! You know I can't! He's not – well, he's not gay, is he?"

"How should I know?" I said. I was cross. "I didn't know *you* were gay. Nor did you until a few weeks ago."

Will looked worried. "Are you mad at me, Natalie? Have I done something?"

I gave a sigh. "No. I'm not mad at you. Sorry. I guess I'm just a bit freaked out. You being gay, I mean. It's a big change."

"I know." He looked down. "I'm sorry. You're being such a good friend."

"Stop saying that," I said.

"But you are. You're the only one I can talk to."

I made an excuse and walked away. I had to, before Will could see how much I was hurting.

There was a real sharp pain, inside me – like I'd been stabbed. I wanted him so much, but he didn't have a clue. He needed me to support him while he was working things out. But all I could do was get upset that he was in love with someone else.

We were both unhappy.

And then Will went and did the worst possible thing.

Chapter 6

Out!

It was the end of PE. The girls had been playing netball. The boys had been playing football. When the bell went, we all started to walk up to the PE block. I looked round for Will and saw him going up to Paul, who was limping at the back of the group.

"What happened to Paul?" I asked one of the boys coming past.

"Got kicked in the shin," he said. "Idiot forgot his shin pads. Gonna have a black and blue leg tomorrow."

I saw Will go up to Paul. He must have been asking if Paul was all right. Paul said something back. Then all of a sudden, Paul took a step back. He nearly fell over. He was staring at Will in horror.

My heart seemed to stop for a moment. Oh, God, no. He wouldn't ...

Paul started running as fast as he could with a bad leg. He banged into the boys who were coming up the path. "Hey!" one of them said. "Watch where you're going!"

"Sorry," I heard Paul say. He was out of breath. "You won't believe what just happened. Will Parsons just asked me out!"

"What?"

"You liar!"

"Never!"

Paul was shaking his head. "No joke. I'm not kidding. He asked me out – just like that."

Everyone started talking and shouting. Most of the boys turned round to look at Will, who was standing right where Paul left him. "Will's gay!" they said. One of them began to laugh.

"Will fancies Paul, Will fancies Paul!" he jeered.

Paul went bright red. "It's nothing to do with me!" he said loudly.

By now the girls had heard too, and they started singing, "Paul and Will sitting in a tree. K-I-S-S-I-N-G ..."

Paul looked angry. "I am *not* gay!"

"Go on, give him a kiss!" said one of the boys.

Paul swore at him. "I am not a bloody fairy, all right?"

"Always knew you were in touch with your female side," said one of the others with a wink.

Paul clenched his fists. "Say that again and you'll be sorry." He nodded his head towards Will. "*He's* the one you should worry about. All of us boys, we're not safe around him. *He's* the one who's gay."

The group turned to stare at Will. "Yeah," said one of the boys. "We shouldn't let him share our locker room."

"I don't want him in there while we're all getting changed," said another. "He could be looking at – you know. Anything."

As I watched them, a ripple of fear seemed to pass over the group. Boys shrank away from Will and began to mutter to each other. "We should speak to the teacher about it ... Can't trust him ... How long's he been like this then? ... He's not sitting anywhere near *me* in the class room ..."

Looking at Will, I felt a sudden rush of pity. He seemed smaller, somehow – as if he'd shrunk. He looked scared, too. Ashamed. Lonely.

"Don't talk about him like that," I said, but it sounded weak. "Being gay isn't a disease."

"That's another thing," said one of the boys. "He's gay. They get AIDS, don't they?"

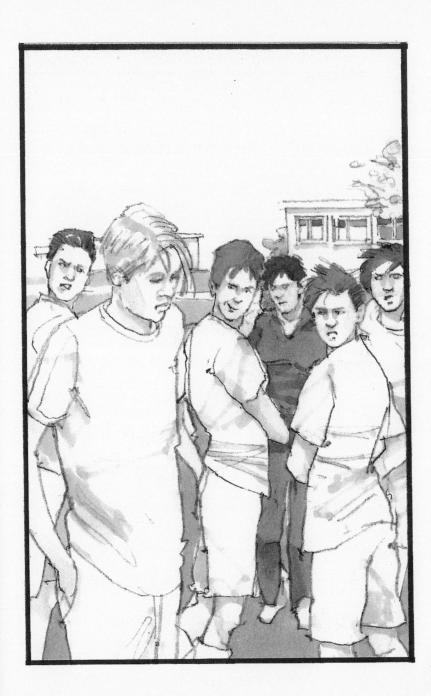

"That's a horrid thing to say!" I said, shocked. But the boy had already turned away.

I saw Paul and moved forward to grab his arm. "He's still Will," I said. "It doesn't mean you can't still be friends."

Paul shook off my hand. He gave me a nasty look as he said, "Get real. I don't want to be friends with a poof." The boys around him were nodding. "Anyway," said Paul, "how do I know he won't try to jump me if we're alone? How do any of us know? I don't want him anywhere near me."

The bell rang again. "Let's get out of here," said one of the boys to Paul. "Get changed and keep him out of the locker room till we're done."

"Yeah. Keep a look out at the door." The group moved off towards the PE block. Every now and then, one of them would look back at Will and mutter something.

Chapter 7

Afterwards

Will had sunk down to the grass. His face was white. Seeing him there, on his knees, I nearly cried. *Why couldn't you have chosen me?* I wanted to wail. *It would have been so easy for you then. See how hard things will be now they all know!*

"I'm glad," Will mumbled as I got to him. "I'm glad they know."

"You're crazy," I said, as I sat down next to him. "You should have kept it a secret."

"No." Will shook his head. "That would be wrong. It's part of who I am. I don't want to be living a lie."

I gave a sigh. "You don't understand. Now you've told them the truth ... your life's going to be so much harder."

Will looked at me, right in the eyes. My heart shuddered. "Do you want me to pretend?" he said softly. "Pretend it's not how I feel?"

Yes, yes, yes! Just keep on pretending, I wanted to say. But even though my heart was thumping, I knew it wasn't the right answer. "No," I said at last. "You have to be true to yourself. I just wish you hadn't done it like that. Everyone knows now. It's going to be all over the school. People will look at you in a different way."

"Not you," said Will, and he smiled at me.

"That's not the same," I said, in a stiff voice. "I'm your friend."

Will took my hand. "You're shaking."

"Of course I am," I said. "That wasn't easy for me either."

He gave a laugh. "Sorry. I'll try not to do it again."

"You won't get a chance," I said. "You're out now. No going back." A tiny flame of hope died inside me.

"Come on then, Carrots," said Will, pulling me to my feet. "Can't sit here all day chatting."

We started back towards the school, and I was thinking, *this is it. From now on, nothing will ever be the same. Nothing.*

Will grinned at me. "All right?"

I grinned back. "Yeah."

I can't ever tell him. He'll never know.

And that's the way it's got to be.

Barrington Stoke would like to thank all its readers for commenting on the manuscript before publication and in particular:

Ann Bailey
Terri Byrne
Jodie Dalziel
A. Godwin
Helga Hughes
Melanie Letheren
Ross Mclaren
Jack Price
Diane Roberts
Rebecca Runciman
Evelyn Smith
Adrianne Sowinski
Dale Steer
Jade White
Simone Wilson

Become a Consultant!

Would you like to be a consultant? Ask your parent, carer or teacher to contact us at the email address below – we'd love to hear from them! They can also find out more by visiting our website.

schools@barringtonstoke.co.uk
www.barringtonstoke.co.uk